One Kiss

The Johnson Sisters Trilogy
Book 3
By Elaine Marie

This is a work of fiction. Names, characters, places, brands, media, and incidents are either the product of the author's imagination or are used fictitiously. Any resemblance to similarly named places or persons living or deceased is unintentional.

Acknowledgments

Special Thanks to:

Andrea Skaar Rott, for all your help and support. We did it!!

Julie Lafrance, for everything!

Stephanie Stacker (Stacker Designs), for creating my beautiful covers.

And to YOU, all my readers. Without your support, these stories would have never been possible. Thank you for your patience. I truly hope you are enjoying them.

Prologue

IT'S BEEN FOUR YEARS since Nicki and Diesel got hitched in Vegas. Three from Jacob and Dani's fairy-tale wedding, and we are now approaching DJ's (David Jacob) second birthday. I've never seen Dani so happy. My nephew is a gift for sure, he is named after his grandpa and daddy, and I adore him.

Two years sure have flown by with DJ. The older I get, the faster the years seem to slip by.

Checking my cell phone for the time, only to discover I have less than an hour to shower and meet the family across town at the carnival to kick off the celebration weekend.

Rushing through my newly decorated apartment, I begin to strip. With my black blouse in hand, I turn and stop short to glare through the bay window.

Professor Fucking Manning.

His living room window faces mine from across the alley. What a sight! Rough around the edges with his lightly bearded face and a small patch of chest hair. His chin lifts, and we make eye contact.

"Fuck!"

I quickly duck away, covering my lace bra with my blouse. Running straight into my bathroom, locking the door behind me. As if someone was chasing me, giggling uncontrollably, "busted!" I say, admitting to myself through the mirror. Tossing my shirt over my shoulder, landing it into the laundry basket.

My face flushed. I dropped my shorts and retreated behind the shower curtain to turn on the water. Once the shampoo and soap are rinsed from my hair, I quickly lather up the body gel and wash the rest of my body. I yank the curtain aside and grab two towels from the shelf above the toilet. One I wrap around my body, the other I use to help dry my hair.

Still thinking of Professor Manning and smiling at how, without knowing, I ended up renting the apartment directly across the way from him. Having , Manning, as a teacher was a pleasure. Now working and living alongside him is starting to take on a life of its own.

Chapter One

Kendra (Keni)

THE CARNIVAL IS ALIVE tonight, the weather is perfect, and the rides are up and running. The music is pumping, and whistles blow loudly from the games.

POP!

I jump back and turn to face the Carni-guy, who's laughing at my reaction as he replaces the dart-stricken balloon.

"Asshole," I throw my middle finger up and continue down the grass path, looking for the kiddy ride section where I'm supposed to meet the family.

"Keni!" I turn to the left and see my parents leaning against the gate, watching alongside Jacob as Dani yells from the ladybug she is sitting in holding DJ. I smile, wave back, and walk over.

"Happy Birthday, DJ!" I call out, resting my arms against the railing. Dani points in my direction, and as he notices I've arrived, he begins to wave. This kid is so freaking spoiled it's ridiculous. Between being the first grandkid, and the first boy, he gets everything and anything he wants. My father was honored. They decided to name David Jacob after him. He's like the son they never had. They love spoiling him, and since they live right across the street, they get to see him daily.

I step to my left to give Mom, Dad, and Jacob a kiss on the cheek, "Hi, where's Nicki and Diesel?" They shrug, knowing she is always late for everything. When the ride ends, Dani and DJ come around the cheap metal fencing, and DJ takes off running with his hands up in the air, right into my arms, as I lift and squeeze.

"Hey Buddy, is today your special day?" I blow kisses on his chubby cheeks. His hair is a chestnut brown, just like his mommy's, and with the sun shining on his eyes, I notice a tint of green. He's going to be a lady killer when he gets older, for sure.

He wiggles down and takes my hand, pulling me toward the fun house across the way.

"Dani, is it okay?" I look back over my shoulder for permission. She nods, "He's been there three times already! Try and keep up," she laughs, taking a deep breath, and I'm sure she appreciates the break.

"DJ, you hold my hand and help me get through, okay?" He glances up and nods his head, "mm-kay." His eyes glare mischievously back at me.

When we reach the top of the third step, he lets go of my hand and takes off running. I watch as he makes it through the shaking shack, following as quickly as I can. His head bobs between the punching bags as the floor shifts from underneath.

"DJ!" I push the last bag aside and hear giggles from the next room. This kid is quick, or I am out of shape? My anxiety begins to spread throughout my body, and I have sweat forming along my hairline.

There are mirrors everywhere. All I see is my reflection. I turn right then left again, only to bump into one and turn to find another. I place my hand out and touch the mirror to help guide myself when I see the little bugger. "DJ, Aunt Keni needs help," I tell him, hoping he'll help me out of this hellhole. I have hated these mazes ever since I was a little kid.

It's all Nicki's fault; she used to get me lost on purpose. I especially hate the corn mazes around Halloween and Thanksgiving because of her. That bitch.

DJ yells back, "NO!" the pitter patter of his feet along the metal grounds get further away. After taking a few deep breaths, I finally make it through and find myself at the slide exit. Thank God.

DJ's giggles come from below, so I know he is on his way down. I slide my legs through the tube and push off for speed. By the time I get to the bottom, the entire family is waiting and, to my surprise, guess who is standing alongside Nicki. None other than Xander.

"DJ, you deserted me!" I pout, trying to cover up the stress I just put myself through. He laughs while holding Dani's hand. I dust my pants off and because my parents raised me right, I greet Nicki and Diesel with, "Hey guys, thanks for joining us."

Nicki reaches out with a hug, "Look who we bumped into in the parking lot, and he's here alone. I told him to tag along if he didn't mind baby crap." I glance in his direction and nod, "Professor Manning. "

"Evening, Miss Johnson, can I speak with you for a moment?" he asks and gestures toward the side of the trailer from hell, "in private?"

I roll my eyes, "We'll catch up," I tell the others to go ahead.

I follow Xander away from the crowd and off to the side. "What's up?" I ask.

"When we aren't at work, I'm Xander. Stop calling me Professor all the time. We are co-workers. I am no longer your teacher in that sense." He seems defeated. I know he's been correcting me and fighting about this for months. But I'm stubborn, and if I give in and he becomes Xander instead of Professor Manning, things can become complicated, possibly even more difficult than they already are.

He continues, "I hate Professor. It makes me feel old. The only reason I use it in class is that it shows they respect me. Clearly, you do not, and you've made that very clear with all your tit-for-tat arguments in class when you were my student. You were the biggest pain in the ass. Do you know that? Questioning everything I discussed, it drove me nuts!" He slides his hands into his front jeans pockets and rocks back on his heels, diverting his eyes away from me. He looks kind of relieved to get all that off his chest.

I open my eyes wide and pull my hand up to cover my mouth. I can't stop the giggle passing through my lips, "Did you just really say tit for tat and then call me a pain in the ass, on top of it?"

Here the sexy uptight man, who was proper and infuriating as my teacher, is just a, normal, down-to-earth guy. Don't get me wrong, I've seen him at the bar here and there, but he has always come across as an uptight, by-the-book kind of person. He is proper, polite and never did I think he would have the balls to confront anyone. I kind of feel bad for him, so I stop giggling.

"Okay, Profess...I mean, Xander. But I can't promise there won't be any more tit for tats." He smirks, slides his hand from his pocket, and we shake on it.

We begin to walk down the path between the games. He stops and pays the carni-guy five dollars to throw a dart. It pops, and he points to the stuffed monkey with purple, spiky hair. When he turns, he hands it to me, "a peace offering?"

"Purple, my favorite color. Thanks." I take the monkey and glance over it while we continue walking to find my family.

"By the way, you may want to invest in some curtains for your bay window," he says. My mouth drops open, the audacity of this guy admitting he saw my tits.

"Growing balls, are we Xander? Don't press your luck," I quickly respond, shaking the monkey and reminding him of the peace offering. But it's too late. My anger builds out of nowhere. How dare he?

"Maybe YOU should get curtains and stop peeking through my windows. I have nothing to hide. It's my apartment, and I can do what I want." The blood in my veins feels like it's boiling, and I walk faster to get away, glancing left and right to find my sisters.

One minute 'mister nice guy, let's be friends.' Next, he thinks he will tell me what to do. I don't think so. I feel him run up beside me. His hand takes my wrist, pulling slightly, "Hey!" he says, I spin to face him.

"How dare you..." I lift my loose hand to strike him, but he catches it, preventing contact.

"I didn't mean any harm," he releases both hands and, with guilt in his eyes, he turns and walks away.

"What was that all about?" Nicki comes up behind me, and I take a deep breath, "Nothing, fucking nothing." Annoyed with myself and with him for putting his hand on me. But guilt-stricken because he doesn't know why I reacted the way I did.

She throws her arm around my shoulder, "It can't be easy."

I turn and look at her, "What?"

She continues, "You had the hots for him when he was your teacher. Now you've been working with him and live right next door. Either you got over it, or you are a hot mess."

I glare through the crowd and see the back of Xander's head as he walks through the exit gates.

A complete hot mess.

Chapter Two

SITTING ON THE COUCH, I reach up to dim the lights and glance out the window. Not one light has been on in his house for two days now. I open my laptop to grade a few essays before turning in for the night. My email pings, Message from *Professor Manning.*

What can this be about? I click on the envelope icon.

Miss Johnson,

Tomorrow (Friday) at eight AM sharp, report to my office.

Oh, shit. What did I do? I've never been asked to come to his office in the past. Work has always been sent electronically, or I pick it up in the bin on top of the filing cabinet at the end of the day. I click on reply and type:

Confirmed.

I finish the last read-through of the essay and close my laptop. The clock on the cable box shows it's after midnight. I stretch my arms out above my head and yawn, "Time for bed."

My laptop is plugged in to charge, and I turn off the light on the end table. The room goes dark, and as I walk past the bay window, I notice a light on next door. I stop in the shadows to see if there is any movement when suddenly he appears.

He looks stressed, holding what I assume is a cup of coffee. Shirtless and in a pair of gray sweatpants. Damn.

Needless to say, I barely slept. My alarm goes off, and I drag myself from under the comforter. Shuffling my feet across the room to start getting ready for work, I reach and turn the radio on to listen for the weather as I grab a towel off the shelf above the toilet and take a quick shower.

Once I'm dressed and ready for the day, I unplug the laptop and grab a to-go coffee cup. With my keys in hand, I turn the lock for the front door and let it close behind me. Off to school, still wondering why Professor Manning has called me to his office so early.

Fifteen minutes later, I am standing outside his office door. It's locked, and the lights are off. I guess he isn't here yet.

I lean against the wall and pull my phone out to check for messages.

"Excuse me, Miss Johnson. I apologize for being late. I missed the bus this morning." He steps past and unlocks the door, walking in as he flips the switch for the lights.

His bag lands on the desk with a thump, and he looks up. "Please close the door and take a seat," he motions toward the two leather chairs in front of his desk.

I do as he asks and sits in the chair closest to the door, dropping my backpack on the floor next to me.

"Well, it's eight AM, not sharp. Why am I here an hour before classes start?" I lean back, throwing a little attitude his way for being late, and cross my arms.

"Actually, Kendra," he says.

So, this is not a formal meeting?

"Yes, Xander?" I cock my eyebrow up in challenge. He can't help but sit back and chuckle.

"Tit for tat, huh?" he replies, trying to wipe the smile from his face. Some of the tension I was feeling alleviated.

"I called you here this morning to apologize. I believe I may have crossed a line when I put my hands on you, and I didn't mean any harm. I wanted to make sure you were okay and wasn't sure you would give me the time of day if I knocked on your door." He leans forward, placing his elbow on the desk. Concern and guilt are written all over his face. It makes me feel bad for the way I reacted.

Relief floods through me like a tidal wave, "I thought I was getting fired," I blurt out. He throws his head back and laughs, "Kendra, why would you think such a thing?"

"I don't know, I guess, after how I acted the other night," I confess and ease myself back into the chair, a little more relaxed. I think it's time we discussed why I reacted the way I did.

"Xander, don't take it personally. I just don't like people grabbing me. The reaction to hit first, and ask questions later, is something I'm working on. It's a Johnson thing." Not embarrassed. It's just the way we were raised.

Always stand up to your bully, speak how you feel, and fuck what anyone else thinks. Take no shit and leave no prisoners. The bigger they are, the harder they fall and all that nonsense. It is what it is.

"I was bullied a lot when I was a kid. Walking away has become my defense mechanism for everything," he admits.

"I'm sorry you went through any of that." I try to make him feel better, and he sighs.

"So, we're good?" He turns in his chair and asks.

I stand up and reach my hand out, "Yes, Xander, and to make it up to you, my place at eight PM sharp tonight, I insist." We shake, and I excuse myself to prepare the classroom for his discussion group.

Chapter Three

I PULL UP ONTO CEDAR Lane, and it begins to rain, just my luck. I park on the opposite side of the street, and as soon as the car door closes behind me, thunder crashes and the rain comes down in buckets. Without hesitation, I dash across the street and straight to the front door of the Wig Wam. I yank the heavy wood door open and walk through the curtain, dripping wet.

Goosebumps form immediately. My nipples harden, and I cross my arms quickly. The cool air is not helping, especially since my t-shirt is soaked.

"Keni, take a table. I'll be back in a minute," Nicki calls out from behind the bar, and I walk past the few regulars and slide into the back corner booth.

"Here," Nicki throws a dry shirt at me. I grab it and jump up from the booth to go around the corner to the lady's room.

I use the hand blower to dry my hair and then change my shirt. When I return, Diesel comes from the kitchen with a plate of fries and a sampler platter.

With a kiss on my cheek, he places them on the table, and Nicki shuffles over with two beers.

"How was work?" She asks, taking a seat. It must be her break time.

"Fun, we get to do it again on Monday," I say sarcastically. She slides the plate in front of me, offering some of her fried food platter.

"No thanks, I have plans. I do need to place an order before I go, however," I admit and sip my beer.

"We were slow earlier. Hopefully, it will pick up tonight." She eats, and we bullshit for a little bit. Then I place my order and have another beer at the bar while I wait for the food.

Diesel is working tonight, and he initiates small talk, still wondering why I chose to move out on my own, thinking he has a say, being my big brother-in-law.

"I don't know why you are in such a rush. Home is free. Free is good. You are still so young. What do you need your own place for anyway?" Nicki starts to laugh at his questions.

"Well, maybe because I'm almost twenty-five, and it's time. Maybe because I need space, or maybe I don't want my father walking in on me when I have a dildo shoved up my hoo-ha!" I threw my hands in the air, giving up on the conversation.

That's right, it happened, and I was mortified. Diesel's eyes get big, his face turns bright red. "TMI, Keni. I should not be hearing these things about my little sister. I'm sorry I asked." He picks up a napkin and waves it in surrender.

The kitchen bell rings. "Saved by the bell!" he says, walking from behind the bar and grabbing the bag with my salads and appetizers.

"Dinner for two?" Nicki asks, smiling.

"Nah, I figure I'll have some for lunch tomorrow." I lean in for a kiss goodbye. No way am I telling her I invited Xander over. Luckily, when I step outside, the rain has subsided enough, and I don't have to run.

It's almost eight, and I have to admit that I'm a little anxious about having Xander in my home. I fluff the pillow on the couch one more time and then hear the knock at the door.

I glance toward the kitchen clock, eight o'clock. The dinner plates are in the oven keeping warm. A bottle of red wine is on the table, and beer is in the fridge.

With one last deep breath, I turn the knob and pull open the door.

White shirt, folded sleeves, pulled up a quarter of the way. Black jeans and a pair of white leather sneakers. Damn.

"Come on in, Profess...Xander," I catch myself.

He brings his arm from behind his back and hands me a bouquet of flowers. Surprised because, well, this is not a date, right?

I reach out, accepting them, "I was taught to never go anywhere empty-handed." I nodded with appreciation, "They are beautiful, thank you," and stepped aside for him to enter.

"Let me get these in some water, make yourself comfortable." I excuse myself to the kitchen and grab a vase from under the sink, fill it halfway with water, add the flowers, and place them in the center of the table alongside the wine.

When I return, he is still standing, "I said to make yourself comfortable," I gesture to the couch. He sits and rubs his hands on the front of his thighs. I sit next to him, "Did you want to watch some T.V., or are you here to eat and run?" I say jokingly.

"If I'm honest, I'm not sure." He rubs his hands again nervously.

"I won't bite, well, not unless you want me to," I whisper, lean back against the couch, grab the remote, and turn on the television.

✳ ✳ ✳

XANDER

What the fuck is wrong with me? I can't stop sweating. I'm nervous as hell. It's just dinner.

"You insisted I come for dinner, so here I am." I sit forward and intertwine my fingers feeling restless.

"And you were on time. Are you hungry because it is ready," she states, lifting herself from the couch and walking toward the kitchen? Her cotton fabric dress nicely hugs all her curves, leading my eyes to the exposed skin which has been kissed by the sun this past summer.

I take a deep breath, stand and run my hand through my hair, "I appreciate it, but maybe I should leave. We really shouldn't be doing this."

"What exactly should we not be doing?" She pulls a plate from the oven, then the other, placing them on the table.

"Co-workers can eat together, can't they?" she asks, and if she didn't look so innocent, I'd swear she was the devil herself.

Maybe she is.

I smirk, feeling embarrassed, and walk into the kitchen. I pull out the chair for her to sit, then walk around the table.

"Yes, we can," I say, taking the seat across from her. "It smells amazing," I admit as she hands me a small bowl with an antipasto salad. An appetizer platter of mozzarella sticks, garlic knots, potato skins and fried zucchini sticks sits to the side. I place the salad bowl to the right of the main course, chicken parmigiana with linguini.

"You made all this?" I ask, lifting my fork and pulling the salad closer.

"I had a little help," she places a black olive in between her lips and sucks it into her mouth.

"From whom?" I ask, curious who the cook in her family may be. When I look up, I have no choice but to swallow hard, watching her lick the oil from her plump lips.

"The Wig Wam and Vitale's," she says, smiling. She glances down, picks up her napkin, and covers her mouth. We both laugh at her admission of not being a cook, and all the tension in the room subsides.

* * *

KENI

After dinner, we sat and had coffee while watching a sitcom. He soon excused himself to get home and grade papers, giving me the night off from doing the boring task.

"I appreciate the night off. This was fun. Thank you for coming." I lean in, kiss his cheek, and hold the door open as he steps through the archway.

"It was. Thank you for having me. Since you paid for dinner tonight, the next time, it's on me." With a wink, he walks down the few steps, up the sidewalk, and to the right.

Next time?

Chapter Four

THE WEEKS ARE FLYING by. I can't believe fall is in full swing. Before you know it, winter will be here. Halloween is tomorrow already, and I can't decide if I want to be sexy, scary, or cute. I look through the catalog and turn the page until I see the perfect costume.

My parents volunteer at the farmers market, where people dress up and go around scaring the kids in the corn mazes. Afterward, we usually end up at the Wig Wam, or I find a party.

This year I didn't make any plans. Between work, editing papers, and trying not to complicate my friendship and co-worker status with Xander, it's been hard.

The scarecrow costume will be perfect. A little revealing in some parts but acceptable to wear around children.

I click on the "buy now" button and arrange to pick it up in-store. The email receipt says it will be ready between five and seven tonight, and I will receive a text message. I glance at the clock on the cable box to check the time. It's still early. I look toward the bay window, hoping to get a glimpse of Xander. No luck.

With my phone in hand, I shoot him a text: *Halloween plans?*

He replies, *None*

I click on the call button, hear the line connect, and he answers after the second ring.

"Hey, I'm stopping by the farmers market tomorrow night and probably going to grab something to eat afterward. Want to come?" I ask, getting up from the couch and walking to the kitchen to get a drink.

"What's at the farmers market?" He asks.

I roll my eyes, "ghost goblins and a corn maze."

The line is quiet for a moment, "do I need to get dressed up?"

"Duh, it's Halloween, of course!" I reply, unaware how anyone can go through Halloween without a costume.

"I don't know," he says.

"Come on, Xander, what else are you going to do?" I convince him to come and tell him to be ready at five tomorrow, "no ifs ands or buts about it."

After disconnecting the call, I dash into my room and throw on a pair of leggings, an oversized shirt, and my comfort clothes. I'll pick up the costume, grab a slice of pizza from the Coliseum and retreat back for some TV time.

The next day- Halloween

The scarecrow costume is cute. I like the way it looks. But it's not the orange and purple one I originally wanted. That one was out of stock, but I'll make the best of it. What do you expect when trying to get a costume the day before Halloween?

The patched-up blue and green dress has matching knee-high socks, a belt, and a tattered hat. It's a raggedy look that I'll spice up by putting my hair in two braids and wearing my high heels.

After adding blush to my cheeks and drawing on a nose, I hear a knock at my door. I pucker my lips to blend the lipstick and yell, "Come in!"

Xander enters, and I can't help but stand in shock. He's also wearing a scarecrow costume "Great minds think alike," he says, turning in place.

I follow suit and spin, "It looks so cute on you," I tell him and grab my phone to take a photo. The oversized overalls are the same blue and green patched design.

"Let's go," I grab my keys, and we drive across town. After finding a parking spot, we climbed out of the car and searched for my parents. Before we get through the haunted house entrance, I hear my mom's voice.

"Oh my! Aren't you two the cutest!" She walks over, leans in, and gives us both a kiss on the cheek.

"Hi, mom. This wasn't planned. It just happened." I state, shrugging, not looking for her to read any more into it than a coincidence, which is exactly what it was.

"Things happen for a reason," she says, as she points to her right. "Dad is already in the maze with his strobe light and chain saw. Have fun!" she says and continues on her way with a bucket of apples.

"Bye, Mrs. Johnson," Xander says, nodding toward the entrance for me to follow.

God, I hate this shit.

We begin to walk through the haunted house. I jump a few times and grab Xander's hand as we reach the end. I know the only way out is by going through the fucking corn maze.

All the memories come flooding in. All the times Nicki enjoyed scaring me with Dad, and the time she left me, I couldn't find my way out.

"Are you all right?" Xander's voice brings me back to the present. I stand there trying to find the courage and not be the chicken-shit little girl I used to be.

"I hate these," I admit, taking a deep breath.

He tightens his grip on my hand, "Concentrate on me. We got this." I watch as he steps forward, and I turn all my attention to him, not taking the chance to look around at the tall hay bales.

I look for anything to distract myself, the way the straw hangs from his hat. How I feel safe holding his hand. The smile of courage and support when he turns back to check on me and the way his arm muscles tighten, pulling me closer.

Safe, that's how I feel whenever I spend time with him. Before I realize it, we are walking toward the exit sign.

He stops and puts both hands on my face, "You made it," he says with a smile, and his thumb rubs along my cheek.

"We made it," I step forward, placing my hand at the back of his neck and pulling him closer with a kiss.

"Thank you."

I take his hand in mine, and we find the nearest path to the parking lot. After finding the car, we remove our straw hats and drive back across town.

Once we arrive at the bar, we take a booth in the back and order food. While we wait, we make small talk about some of the students and the upcoming holiday season.

I showed him a few pictures Dani sent of DJ in his costume. As usual, the whole family costume thing is going on.

Jacob was dressed as Homer, Dani as Marge with tall blue hair, and DJ made the cutest Bart Simpson ever.

"I like how you and your family are so close. I didn't have that growing up," Xander says, placing an empty plate to the side and wiping his face with a napkin.

"Where did you grow up?" I ask, wondering why we never really talk about his past. You would think by now I'd know more about him.

"Here and there, Pennsylvania mostly." He leans back in the booth and relaxes after finishing his open-sliced steak sandwich and fries.

Are we dating? Not really. We are friends and co-workers, and we hang out more than ever. But at the end of the day, all we ever seem to do is kiss.

"Any plans for the holidays?" I ask, offering him the last potato skin from the sampler platter. He shakes his head, and I place it on my appetizer plate and add ranch dressing to dip it.

"I'm not going anywhere, no family-no place to go." He shrugs it off as if it's no big deal. To me, family is everything. I feel bad he didn't have the same safe family life I grew up with.

"Well, we are your family now. So, you'll spend it with us." I bite, and the creamy ranch dressing drips, covering my lip. Before I get a chance to lick it or grab my napkin, Xander reaches over and wipes it away.

He lifts his thumb to his mouth and licks.

Hot Damn.

Chapter Five

T*hanksgiving day*

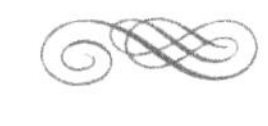

I PULL UP TO MY PARENTS' house and glance across the street to Dani and Jacob's as they come walking across the driveway. Beside them is Xander with DJ on his shoulders. He has become one of the family, and I must say, watching him laugh and play with DJ has shown a softer side of him. He is definitely going to be a good father one day.

"Hi guys," I says, closing my car door with the bag containing the salad and platter tray.

"Happy Thanksgiving," they say, and Dani leans in for kisses. DJ leans down and messes with my hair.

"I'm a turkey. Gobble, gobble, gobble!" he says, and Xander puts his hands out, gesturing to take the trays from me. I shake my head, letting him know I've got it, "a turkey, well! I'm going to eat you up!" I playfully lean in and naw on DJ's leg.

He giggles and squirms, almost sliding off of Xander's shoulders.

Jacob holds the front door open while we all walk through. Mom, of course, is in the kitchen, and dad is relaxing on the couch. Nicki and Diesel are out on the back deck, filling the cooler with some type of alcohol. I slide the platter and tray into the fridge and look into the oven.

"That's a big bird!" I swipe my finger in the mashed potato bowl and lick. "Smells good, mom," I plant a kiss on her cheek and sit at the table to help prep the utensils.

Once I have the fork, knife, and spoon in the napkin, I fold it and move on to the next.

"You'll never guess who will be joining us," Mom says, pushing the potatoes into a tin. Thanksgiving is a major thing here in the Johnson household. She makes so much, we put everything in tins and do buffet style.

"Who?" I wonder, placing the last set of utensils in the basket.

"Brian." I stop short and drop the basket. Sitting at the dining room table with a beer in front of him sits my ex-boyfriend. With a quick turn, I retreat back into the kitchen.

"Why would you invite him?" I mumble, walking past my mom out the back door to grab a beer from the cooler. Ugh, of all people.

"Kendra, I don't understand?" I pop the top off a twisted tea and chug half of it.

"Mom, I broke up with him years ago. Why would you invite him for Thanksgiving dinner?" I pull the chair out and sit. The air is crisp with a chill. The temperature is dropping.

"I bumped into him at the market this morning, he is all alone, and Thanksgiving is for all. I thought things ended well. No hard feelings."

"For fuck's sake, mom. That doesn't mean I want to spend the holidays with him." I look on the table to see what bottle

I'll take a shot from. Good old Nicki never disappoints. Fireball it is.

"Kendra, you know our door is always open to everyone," Mom says, turns, and goes back inside. How am I going to deal with mister *'you don't break up with me. I break up with you'*?

Especially now that Xander is here, and we have been flirting back and forth for months.

I think for another moment, finishing my Tea, "it'll be fine. You're right mom Thanksgiving is for all, and I am thankful for you." I say out loud for no one to hear.

Besides, I think to myself. Maybe this will light a fire under Xander to finally make a move. How can I use this to my advantage? I take another moment before returning, and when I do, I have a beer for Xander and a full Tea in hand for myself.

"Hi, Brian. Have you met Xander?" I ask, sitting between the two men at the table. Brian leans in to kiss my cheek. I pull back, dismissing him. Xander moves his chair closer and places his arm over my shoulder.

Hmm... jealousy is a bitch.

"Yes, a professor. Your Professor and boss?" Brian asks, sitting back in his chair, annoyed and glaring toward me as if he has any claim on me.

"And neighbor," I add with a smile and sip my Twisted Tea. I think I'm going to need something stronger. As if my sister, Nicki, read my mind, she places shots of Fireball in front of us. Dani walks over, grabs one, and yells, "Mom, get in here."

Mom comes running, grabs one of the shot glasses from the table, looks around to us all, and holds it up, "Happy Thanksgiving, may we gobble 'til we wobble."

Dani, Nicki, and I raise our glasses and, in sync, yell, "gobble, gobble, gobble!" and down the shots. DJ comes galloping through the room, mimicking us, gobble, gobble, gobble, and disappears into the other room.

"Dinner is served," Dad brings the turkey tray and places it on the rack. Everything is perfect until Brian bluntly suggests he and I go for a walk alone afterward.

"Look here, Brian," I lean in closer so only he can hear. "You eat my mother's home cooking, say thank you, and then leave. You may have been invited, but you are not welcome, as far as I am concerned." I pull back, put my plate on the table and walk into the kitchen.

Xander walks through the doorway and out to the deck, and I follow.

"Hey, everything okay?" I ask, opening the cooler for him.

"No, I should go," he says.

"Why?" I wonder, grabbing another drink for myself. "We're going to head over to Dani's for drinks and games."

He turns, looks through the window, then back at me.

"Is Brian going?" his eyes narrow, with aggravation shining through his eyes. Is he irritated and jealous?

"Xander, we've been over for a long time, and I won't go back. If I break it off with someone, it's over. I do not repeat my mistakes." I pull my sweater closed as the cold air attacks my exposed skin.

Looking more relieved, he asks, "Drinks and games?" I shake my head. He steps closer and places his hands on my arms, rubbing up and down, trying to help keep me warm.

"Adult drinks and games," I confirm with a wink, turn on my heel and go back into the house.

"Mom, are you sure you don't want help cleaning up?" I ask, placing the tin on the kitchen counter. "No, no. DJ is already asleep on Pop Pop's lap. You kids, go have fun!" She pulls the tin lids from the pantry and begins to cover the leftovers.

Nicki wheels the cooler through the back door, and Diesel isn't far behind with two full bags of liquor bottles. Brian steps into the kitchen and clears his throat, looking from Xander to me, and then focusing on my mother.

He thanks her for dinner, refuses a pre-made take-home tin, tucks his hands in his pockets, and walks out with his head down. Bye, Brian.

Dani kisses DJ on the forehead, say goodnight, and takes Jacob's hand to walk out the front door.

Chapter Six

THE FIREPLACE IS LIT, and the table is covered with empty bottles, "Never have I ever." Nicki yells, and I roll my eyes. "Okay, okay!"

Drunk Dani laughs. It's good to see her having fun and not worrying about DJ.

"What's that?" Xander asks.

I explain, "Never have I ever - game." I removed a few bottles from the table and replaced them with full ones.

"Okay, so like, I would say: Never have I ever passed out at a bar. Now, if you have done it, you have to drink. If you haven't done it, you don't." He nods, understanding the rules.

Dani starts, "Never have I ever woken up in a stranger's bed." I leave my drink in hand. Nicki snarls and drinks and so does Diesel. I can't help the laugh that escapes. These two are made for each other.

"Never have I ever... Oh, fuck, this game sucks." Nicki says, slurring her words. "Yeah, because there isn't much you haven't done." Diesel says, laughing.

"Okay, okay," I interrupt. "Never have I ever had sex in a kitchen." I blurt out and look around the circle witnessing Jacob, Dani, Nicki, and Diesel drink.

Xander doesn't.

Nicki leans forward, "Never have I ever had sex in a car."

"Okay, Nicki, that's a lie," Diesel says when he lifts his drink, we all follow except for Xander.

Huh.

"Never have I ever had sex in a closet," Dani says. Nicki drinks and I ask, "How did this become an all-about sex game?" We continue around the room, and everyone's feeling pretty good. But I notice Xander doesn't drink on any of the sex statements.

Then I think he has to drink on this, "Never have I ever had sex in a bed."

All eyes go to Xander as he runs his hand through his hair, his face flush, but he leaves his drink down.

"What the hell, Xander? Have you never had sex?" Nicki blurts out, and I'm surprised at her coming across so vile. It's none of our business, yet I can't stop looking to him for the answer. It's there written in his eyes... he hasn't.

He sighs and leans back on the couch, crossing his legs, "No."

The room goes silent, nobody knowing what to say. Leave it to Nicki to break the silence.

"Well, Keni, you better rectify that situation," she says, and I'm all for it, but, "Seriously, Nicki?" I glare toward her, feeling the embarrassment coming from Xander.

Being the mature one, Dani sees how uncomfortable we are all becoming and changes the subject, taking the attention off of Xander and me.

"Let's play cards." She pushes up from the floor where she is sitting between Jacob's legs and opens the drawer. She grabs a deck of cards and tells us to come into the dining room to sit at the table.

"I appreciate you letting us crash, but I think I will make a cup of coffee," I tell Dani. She nods, understanding I won't be staying. I can't expect Xander to spend the night here after Nicki outing him and making him uncomfortable.

We play a couple of rounds of poker while I have my coffee, "I think I'm going to get ready to go. It's late, Xander. Do you want a ride home?" I offer lifting myself from the table and bring my mug to the kitchen.

"I don't know. Are you going to take advantage of me?" He follows. Not that it hasn't crossed my mind, I look over my shoulder toward him.

"Get him!" Nicki slurs while climbing on top of Diesel's lap.

"I love you all, but I'm leaving." I grab my bag and get my keys making my way around the table, saying goodnight, then we walk to the door.

"Text me when you get in," Dani says. Xander waves goodnight and helps me with my jacket.

We don't exchange any words for the fifteen-minute drive home. Once I park in front of my apartment, I have to ask, "Are you really a virgin?"

I don't dare look at him, "you don't have to answer that. It's none of my business that was rude. Sorry." I pull the lever to open the door and get out.

I reach the sidewalk when he climbs from the car, "I am," he says and walks towards his door.

Well, holy fuck!

This explains so much. All the flirting, yet we've only kissed. All the attraction, then a distraction. This just became so much more complicated.

Chapter Seven

A *few weeks later.*

WHILE SITTING IN THE back corner of the classroom, I admire the professor who has been keeping his distance as he paces back and forth summarizing the semester. We'll take a short winter recess, and then it will start back up again in April. During that time, we go over all the new regulations and research how to better reach students. We'll also have meetings and communications with fellow teachers to collaborate on lesson plans.

"There are no words to express my gratitude for the privilege to have been your professor for this class. I know it may sound like bullshit, but it is sincere. I get to teach what I love alongside one of the best Teacher Assistants, Miss Johnson, and that makes me a very lucky man." Xander says, "Can we have a round of applause for Miss Johnson and all her help this semester?" He begins clapping, and the embarrassment creeps into my face. I stand, bow and make my way to the front of the class.

"Thank you, Professor Manning. It has truly been an honor grading all your papers," I put my hands out in front of me, acknowledging the students. Then I turn and continue, "And doing all your work for you this semester," I say, a big smile on my face, and some of the students laugh.

"But honestly, each and every one of you has inspired me to continue on my journey. Each of you can be whatever you want to be. Make every day count, even the hard ones. Lessons learned are the most valuable. Now, get the heck out of here!" I clap for the students as they walk down, say their goodbyes, and exit the classroom.

Once the classroom is empty, I slide my laptop into my backpack. "Come into the office for a celebratory drink?" Xander asks. I nod and follow him through the door, down the hall and wait as he unlocks his office.

I close the door behind me and take a seat. He pulls a bottle with two glasses from his desk.

"I was thinking, instead of coming to the office, since we live right next to each other, can't we just stay home and do all this meeting bullshit in our pajamas?"

He slides a glass across the desk. I reach over and grab it.

I'm trying to get back the friend I seem to have lost at Thanksgiving. Don't get me wrong, we talk, but since that night, we have not flirted, and if I'm honest. I miss his kiss, just one more kiss.

* * *

XANDER

Spending time off campus in our pajamas? Is she nuts?

I can see the benefit of not having to get on the bus and drag my ass into the office daily, but I'm not sure about this.

"It may be doable, but you'll have to wear clothes. I've seen your pajamas. They are not acceptable for work," I state, remembering what she looks like in her sleepwear.

She sits back in the chair, "Still peeking through my windows, are you?" she says, holding out her glass. "May we live to learn well, and learn to live well," she toasts.

I hold my glass up, but before clicking, I say, "Drink to life and the passing show and the eyes of the prettiest girl I know." The glasses make contact. She blinks her eyes rapidly, tilting her head to the right and acting bashful. It's the cutest thing, with her long brown hair cascading over her shoulders and her plump thick, succulent lips touching the brim of the glass.

Fuck, fuck, fuck!

I drink and sit forward on the chair, grabbing the bottle and offering another to Kendra. "No, thank you. I need to get home and then head over to the Wig Wam. I promised Diesel and Nicki I would help set up the holiday decorations.

"You should stop by if you're not doing anything. I can always drive you home afterward." she offers, and I may take her up on that offer.

Chapter Eight

KENI

IT'S TWO WEEKS UNTIL Christmas, and the holiday carols are already getting on my nerves. I pull the light strands from the box and take the staple gun with me to the dining area where Diesel stands, trying to figure out what else to do.

On the back table is a garland, "I'm thinking of wrapping the garland with the lights and going around the ceiling edges."

He agrees, "I'll go get the ladder. Nicki should be back with another round of drinks in a minute."

I begin to intertwine the lights with the green garland, and every two feet, I add a red bow.

"Wow, you're good at this." Xander walks toward the table and points to the hanging decorations.

I smile, "Thanks, I enjoy it." I stop to take a sip of my drink and place the pint glass back onto the table, out of the way. When Diesel returns with the ladder, Xander offers to help.

"Now that I have all this put together, it will be easier," I say, laying the garland along the length of the back room. Nicki runs back with a couple of shots, "Looking good, kiddo!" she says, handing me the tray.

"Thanks for your help, Professor," she turns back toward the bar. I place the tray on the side table, "It's Xander. His name is Xander," I call out, wiping my mouth and shaking off the burn from the fireball shot. Nicki looks over her shoulder and smiles, "Xander, it is, then."

* * *

XANDER

It seems she's been drinking all afternoon, but who am I to judge? I am the one who sits behind the desk, sulking with a bottle of my own.

She grabs the open ladder and yanks it toward the wall. I can't believe she thinks she is sober enough to climb up the ladder without any help or support. She is the most stubborn woman I have ever met.

Before I can open my mouth to protest, she bites down on the strand of garland wrapped in lights and climbs, approaching the top at record speed. In two quick strides, I am underneath her, holding the metal ladder in place.

"Um, Kendra, are you sure this is a good idea?" I ask, trying to hold the ladder not looking at her beautiful plump ass staring back at me.

"I got this," she mumbles through her closed teeth, "hand me the staple gun," she says. I reach down and grab it from the table. Without looking up, I held it high for her to grab.

The next thing I hear is the gun going off, "Okay, slide me over," she says. I take the chance and look up, "What? I am not sliding the ladder over while you're up there. You'll fall!" I let go and placed my hands on my hips, protesting.

"Pussy," she calls out and starts to climb down. When she gets to the third step, I grab the ladder, "Hold on," and slide it four feet to the left so she can go back up again. We repeated this around the dining room until we came to the door frame.

Once she finished stapling the last part, she climbed down and turned to face me. My hands are still on the ladder, closing her in.

"Don't ever call me a pussy, again," I stare straight into her dark brown eyes. The urge to lean in and kiss her is overwhelming.

I watch as she swallows hard, "Okay, sorry... I was joking," comes out between her lips in a slow and choppy whisper.

"Who needs a drink?" Nicki interrupts and places fresh glasses on the table.

"Diesel, I think we're done with the ladder," I say and drop my arms to allow Kendra to move. She squeezes between me and the ladder, rubbing ever so gently against my groin, for the love of God.

***

KENI

My heart is racing. Being so close to his hard body makes my insides go haywire. Maybe it's the alcohol, maybe it's how we've gotten close over the last couple of months, or maybe it's just that I'm done waiting.

We've been having a casual conversation all night. That is until I pissed him off. Not that it matters, but I was joking when I called him a pussy. I didn't mean any harm. It was a challenge. I didn't think he could do it, and yet he did.

When I climbed down, and his arms closed in on the ladder, trapping me, his face mere inches from mine, it's when I knew.

I should have leaned slightly forward and kissed him, one kiss.

Nicki nudges me from the side, "Can you come help me?" she asks, and I follow her to the back hall by the bathrooms. I'll do anything to distract myself from wanting to throw Xander down on the table and fuck him hard.

"Are you okay?" she wonders, and if I'm honest, "I'm buzzed. But I need more." She nods, "Sit at the bar," I'm instructed, but head into the bathroom to freshen up.

Once I plant my ass on the bar stool next to Xander, two shots and a beer chaser are placed in front of me. What looks like water in a pint glass rests by Xander.

"Are you quitting on me?" I question, grab a shot, and down it.

"If you'd like, I can drive your car home so you can enjoy the evening." He offers, I reach back to locate my keys, but they're not in my back pocket. I look around and then hear the jingle of them being shaken. Xander holds them out and shakes them again.

I shrug my shoulders, "Okay," and down the other shot, then chase it with the beer. Music is playing, and as I glance at the television, we hold a light conversation about the students this past semester.

When it's time to go, I stand and sway, "Well, shit..." I giggle, grabbing hold of the stool. Xander being the gentleman he is, reaches out, giving me his arm for support. Diesel asks if I'm okay, and Nicki follows us out of the bar.

"You sure you got her?" I hear her say. Xander helps me into the passenger seat of my car.

"I promise I'll have her text you once she is home safe," he replies.

"Thanks, we appreciate you looking out for her." The door closes, and I can't hear anything else.

My head is spinning. I need to get home. I lean over and reach for the steering wheel from the passenger seat when the driver's side door opens, "Hey, what do you think you're doing?" Xander says, pushing my hand away, and sits down, places the key in the ignition, and starts the engine.

"Home, I need to get home," I tell him, resting my head against his shoulder and placing my hand on his thigh.

Chapter Nine

XANDER

WE DIDN'T EVEN MAKE the turn-off on Cedar Lane before she passed out. I glance down and kiss her forehead after the car is parked, and I turn the engine off. I sit in the driver's seat debating, wondering, and fighting internally with myself. She is beautiful, bright, and a smart ass, and I would do anything for her. If she only knew that I have been waiting for someone like her all my life.

Someone sweet, honest, and loyal, and her family is the typical all-American family. Down to earth would go out of their way for you. Don't get me wrong, I've seen these Johnson sisters kick ass and stand up for each other. It's something I didn't have growing up.

She begins to move. I quickly get out of the car, run to the passenger door, and open it. She pushes herself out and right into my arms. I help guide her up the path and open the door. She stumbles in and falls onto the couch.

I haven't the heart to leave her just yet. I sit in the bulky chair in the corner and watch her chest rise and fall with every breath she takes.

Beautiful, smart, outgoing, and what a mouth on her. She enjoys watching sports, joking around, playing darts, and singing to the jukebox. She's everything I've been waiting for and then some. I check the time on my phone and shoot Nicki a message that Keni is safe. I should head home myself.

I grab the blanket off the back of the couch and cover her. Hoping not to disturb her, I whisper, "one kiss, that's all I'm going to take from you tonight. But one day, I'll give you all of me."

Our lips touch, and she moves slightly opening her lips. I can't stop myself. I slide my tongue in, and her arms wrap around my neck, pulling me closer.

It's overwhelming, the sensations running through my body, instantly making me hard. I need to stop this. She's been drinking, it's not right, and I've...I've never wanted anyone more.

I pull back. Her big brown eyes stare back at me. With a smile, she tugs the blanket, turns to her side, and says, "night Xander."

I gulp down hard, take a deep breath and walk towards the hall, "Goodnight, Kendra," I say. Her beautiful smile is the last thing I see before closing the door.

* * *

KENDRA

The smell of his cologne still lingers in my apartment as I remove myself from the couch and start a pot of coffee. Leaning against the counter, I bring my fingertips to my lips. One kiss, and I wanted him and everything he has to offer in life.

But I couldn't. It wasn't right. Not for his first time, at least.

The first time you have sex should be special. A little romance, some foreplay, and the perfect setting with a person you care about. Not a late, drunk night at a house party on top of a bunch of coats in some stranger's parents' bedroom. Trust me, I know.

I pop the cap off the aspirin bottle and spill two into my palm, taking them with a sip of my coffee. Stepping into the living room, I grab my phone from the table and text Xander.

Thanks for driving us home last night. I owe you. Dinner?

The three dots appear, and he replies: *Are you sure?*

Keni: *I asked, didn't I?*

Xander: *Feeling okay?*

Keni: *Never better.*

Xander: *What time?*

Keni: *seven, we'll "Netflix and chill."*

Xander: ...

Oh man, did I scare him? I mean, I literally just told him I wanted to fuck, right? Shit.

I walk toward the bay window and look across to his apartment. He's pacing back and forth with his phone in hand. He stops, looks over his shoulder, and sees me. His arm lifts the phone to his ear.

My phone rings. I press the green circle to accept the call, "I didn't mean it." I say quickly. Our eyes connect, and I can't look away.

"You didn't?" His voice comes through, distraught.

"I did, but if you don't want to, we don't have to," I admit and bite my lip.

He reaches up and runs his fingers through his hair, "it's sexy as hell when you do that," I whisper.

"Seven o'clock, dinner. I can't promise anything else," He abruptly hangs up and walks out of view.

Damn this man.

Chapter Ten

XANDER

IT'S BEEN A LONG DAY, yet here it is, six forty-five, and I dread the walk over to Kendra's. She wants to *Netflix and Chill*. What the fuck!

How am I supposed to explain? I mean, it's not that I don't want to have sex. MY GOD! I want to, but I've waited this long for the right woman to come along. What if she's not the one?

The dryer buzzer goes off, and I walk towards the small laundry room to retrieve my white dress shirt. The warmth caresses my skin as I slide my arms through and begin to button it closed. Who am I kidding? How is she not the one?

I've taken three showers today in preparation. Rumor has it that the more you jerk off, the better prepared you'll be and the longer you can last when you finally lose your virginity. I'm still not even sure I can go through with it. Will she laugh at me? Will I be any good? Don't get me wrong, I've done things, but this is different. She is different.

We've spent so much time together, between her being my student and teaching assistant and being neighbors. Her family has been genuinely nice and accepting of our friendship; they've even invited me for the holidays.

This is nuts. Why am I even worried?

I grab my jacket from the hook by the front door and throw it on as I pull the door open. It's snowing, and coming down hard, it looks like we'll have a white Christmas after all.

＊＊

KENI

I watch as he walks up the sidewalk, and before he can knock, I pull the door open, "Hurry, it's freezing!" I wave him in and shut the door quickly.

"Why is it so cold in here?" he asks, shoving his hands in his pockets. I push my hood down from my head, "The heat's not working. The landlord said he can't get here until tomorrow afternoon." I tell him, "Maybe we should reschedule this?" I offer. Feeling guilty, I put him on the spot with the whole "*Netflix and Chill*" offer.

"Let me take a look," he says and walks towards the basement door. I have to admit. I only go down there to do laundry; otherwise, no, thank you. It's cold and damp and reminds me of a dungeon.

I follow and flip the switch for the lights to come on.

"Well, the blower is running, but no heat is coming out," he says and starts messing with what I assume is the furnace.

"What does that mean?" I wonder, stepping to the side.

"Basically, the furnace is working, but the filter is probably clogged," He motions toward the small workbench where an old metal toolbox sits. I shrug my shoulders, "Go for it."

He pulls his jacket off, tossing it onto the bench, and begins to fold up his sleeves. Fuck, Nicki was right. That look is sexy as hell. I can feel my inside begin to warm even though the heater isn't fixed. I bite my lip and release, "I appreciate this, but you don't have to. I mean, the landlord is responsible and will be here tomorrow." I explain, feeling bad but enjoying the view.

"Really, Kendra, it's not a problem at all." He walks around the basement, moves a few things, and when he comes back to where I'm standing, he has a rectangular accordion-looking thing in his hand.

"Looks like the landlord stocked up. There are three of them leaning against the wall." He bends down to flip the switch, and the unit goes silent. "First and foremost, always turn the power off." he says, "This prevents any loose dirt or dust from getting into the system."

Ah, so Xander knows a thing about a thing or two. I'm impressed.

..*

XANDER

I pulled the filter from between the return and blower, and it looks like it hasn't been changed in years. Once I place it to the side, I check to see where the airflow arrow is. To make sure I insert it correctly, the red arrow is pointing toward the blower.

"Would you like to do the honors?" I asked, Kendra, pointing to the switch to power up the unit. She smiles, steps forward, and flips it.

The unit kicks in, "I'd leave the old one here for the landlord to see. It should start to warm up now." I walk over and take my jacket from the workbench.

Stepping in front of Kendra, I wrap my jacket and arm around her, "Come on, let's get you warmed up." We walk up the stairs from the basement, and she says, "My thoughts exactly," and all the anxiety returns.

"Kendra," I say, as we reach the top of the stairs, and I turn my back to close the door.

"Xander?" she says, and as I turn to face her, she pushes me back to the door, and her mouth is on mine.

Oh fuck, she tastes like hot cocoa.

Instinctively my hands go to her sides, then up her back. I want more, no, I need more. I've been waiting all day to have just one more kiss.

Her hands move down my sides and towards my cock, yes...yes.

She cups me, and I swear I'm going to come. I push her shoulders back and stare into her eyes.

"Kendra, there's something you should know." I let out between breaths, feeling the distance between us was killing me inside.

She steps back, "Xander, we are not going to have sex tonight." She says, "I didn't mean to put any pressure on you." She moves close, "but we are going to fool around."

I lean down, press my lips to hers, then move to her neck and along her jawbone.

I was going to tell you I love you. I think to myself when she steps to the side, taking my hand in hers and leading us to the couch.

She gently pushes me to sit and climbs on top of my lap. Lips on lips, hands roaming, and my cock growing.

"Is this okay?" she whispers in my ear. "More than okay," I admit and take her mouth again. I'm not sure how much time goes by, but when she lifts herself off my lap and begins to take off her sweatshirt, I stop her.

Not because I don't want to see, touch, or even feel. It's because I want to tell her how I truly feel about her before we do it, and I don't have any condoms. I'm not prepared. Even though internally, I'm ready, it just doesn't feel like the right moment.

"What the fuck?" She yanks the sweatshirt down, her tone so angry, and while she walks away, she says, "Shit, now I can't even get felt up?"

Once I can move, I walk toward the kitchen, where she's sitting on the counter with a mug in her hands.

"Maybe I should go," I don't know what else to say. Am I leading her on without meaning to?

"Good, get the fuck out," she says, not even lifting her face to acknowledge I'm in the same room with her. I don't understand. One minute she is okay with not doing the actual deed. The next, she is furious.

"Kendra, it's not what you think. This has nothing to do with you." I try to explain, but she turns her face away, dismissing me as if I mean nothing. Maybe I don't. Maybe she just needed to get laid.

"This is far from over, that I can promise you," I tell her and grab my jacket from the floor where she dropped it and walk out.

One kiss was all it took for me to fall in love with her. How did I let this happen? I want to give all of myself to her. I've never wanted someone so fucking badly that it hurt.

* * *

KENDRA

One minute he's all in, the next cold as ice. I don't know what his issue is, but I'd be damned if I'm going to sit around any longer waiting for him.

Over five fucking years, almost six fucking years, I've wanted him.

I grab my phone from the counter and text Nicki: *You working?*

She replies with a thumbs up.

Good, because I need to get drunk.

Chapter Eleven

THREE SHEETS TO THE wind, I'm drunk as a skunk and don't even care. I motion for another drink.

"Don't you think you've had enough?" Nicki asks, and I snarl at her, "No, nope, not even close." I lift the glass but somehow miss my mouth and hit my cheek. Beer spills.

"Wet t-shirt party!" I scream out with my pint glass raised.

"No!" Nicki comes around the bar and grabs the glass from me.

"You're a party pooper," I tell her, "What happened to you? You used to be so much fun." I sulk in my own pity.

"Keni, drinking will not change anything. If there is a problem, you need to talk about it," she says, and I wobble my head like a bobble doll and stick out my tongue.

"Talking is overrated. Bring my drink." I turn and stumble towards the back to find an empty booth.

"What has gotten your panties in a bunch?" she asks, sliding my drink across the table.

"Fucking Xander," I stare at the condensation building on the side of the glass.

"Oh?" she leans back to listen.

"He kissed me. I mean, we've kissed – many times but never..." I sigh. It's been amazing. The way he touches me and makes me feel so wanted. One kiss, and I melt and want more. So much more.

"I invited him to Netflix and chill." Embarrassed, I cover my face and peer through my fingers. "That takes balls," she says.

"Yeah, but he freaked out or something. I mean, he came over, but the heat in my apartment wasn't working. He fixed it, and then I kissed him, and I started to rub him, and he pushed me away. FUCK him." I feel the anger begin to build again. After hours of drinking to help release it, it came back full force.

I want to hit something, someone. Nicki waves towards the bar, "the heat's working now?" she tries to distract me, and I nod.

"The uber will take you home, I and Diesel will drop off your car when we are done here. You need to sober up and re-think what took place and how to move forward. I see the way he looks at you. There is something between the two of you." I shrug my shoulders, "Whatever."

Annoyed, I push up from the table and stumble toward the door.

"Be good," someone says. I reply by putting my middle finger up and walking out the door.

Be good, what fun is that?

Chapter Twelve

A GRAY NISSAN PULLS up. I knock on the window, "Are you my uber?" the girl smiles, "I think so. Are you going to Copley?" I nod, reach for the passenger door handle, climb in, and point forward, "Onward!"

It takes about seven minutes to get to Copley Avenue from the Wig Wam, but it felt like forever. I fight with the seatbelt to get out, stumble three steps, and, with help from the slick ice, down I go.

Laughing hysterically, I lay back in the snow, the cold feeling good on my overheated, frustrated body.

"Are you okay?" I hear from the driver. I can't help but continue to laugh, opening my mouth and trying to catch the snowflakes. Sliding my arms back and forth, I begin to make a snow angel.

***

XANDER

She is drunk off her ass, literally. I watch as she slips and falls, and I come running from next door.

"I'll take care of her," I let the uber driver go. It was nice that she was waiting to make sure Kendra got inside, but this might take a while.

"Kendra?" I walk with caution, not afraid to slip but concerned about what her reaction may be toward me. I know when I left earlier, she was angry, but that is partially her fault since she didn't let me explain. All I wanted to do was tell her how much I was in love with her.

"Xander? Xander, is that you?" She tries to get up but slips to the side, laughing. She can't seem to get to her feet. She crosses her legs, "Why don't you want me?" she mumbles.

"Kendra, you have it all wrong." I reach out my hand. She tilts her head up. Her big brown eyes stare back at me, "Let me get you inside," I say, wiggling my fingers out in front of her.

She reaches up as I pull and tug her into me. Instincts have my arms wrapping around her. She leans in, and we kiss, her hands rake down my back, and I pull away. Again.

"You've been out for hours," I push the hair behind her ear, move my finger to her chin and gently push so she'll look me in the eye.

Tears are building, and guilt fills my chest, "I don't mean to hurt you." I kiss the tip of her nose, then rest my lips on her forehead. God, how can I fix this?

"Fuck you, Xander. I'm done," she says, stepping to the side and walking up the path. I turn and watch as she fumbles with her keys but gets inside. I know I'm not welcome with the slam of the door, so I retreat to my own home.

Once I lock my front door, I find myself leaning against the window frame, looking into her living room.

✳ ✳ ✳

KENDRA

I can feel his eyes on me as I lie back on the couch and begin to touch myself. God, how I want him so bad. But he rejected me again; granted, I'm drunk, but shit. If I were a guy with a girl that looked like me throwing herself at me, I'd be all over her.

But no, not Xander.

I slide my hand over my nipple and pinch ever so slightly. Oh, that feels good. I proceed down my torso and let my fingers slide under my buttoned jeans. Fuck how I want his hands on me, his mouth all over me, his cock inside me.

My phone pings and I reach down to grab it from the table. "Show me, teach me." He says, and I'm surprised into a standstill. Voiceless. I mean, it's one thing to know he is watching and not have any communication, but *teach me*?

His words have me glaring out the window. Without missing a beat, I press the speaker, place the phone back on the table and lean back, spreading my legs.

I turn myself on, touching my breast and moving lower, raking my nails on my inner thighs. After I lower my pants, I use my right hand to apply pressure through my panties, letting out a moan.

His breathing becomes labored through the speaker, but no words are shared. In and out, I slide my fingers, then press on the nub while shifting my hips and grinding against my hand. Fuck, I'm coming.

Breathless, I moan, "Xander," and ride out my orgasm and falling back, I close my eyes and fall asleep.

Chapter Thirteen

A *week before Christmas*

NO WORK THIS WEEK. Thank the heavens for small favors. I have to get my ass to the stores and do my Christmas shopping. I still don't know what to get everyone. I put the car in drive and head up to Queen Anne Road. I'll make a right, head to Route Four and hit the mall. When I stop at the red light at the corner of Cedar Lane, my phone rings.

"Hey, Dani, what's up?" I ask and glance to see if the light has changed.

"Just checking in, are we still doing Christmas at Mom and Dad's?" she asks. Since she had DJ, it's seemed easier for us all to exchange gifts there.

"Yes, Ma'am, I'll be there," I tell her and begin to accelerate. "Good, you can drive Xander then?" she asks.

Ugh, I've been trying to avoid him, but, "Yeah, I guess." We disconnect the call, and I wonder where the two of us stand.

Ever since the night he watched me come, we have had little to no contact. Other than the occasional strip tease through the window, I don't know if I scared him or if he didn't like what he saw.

Every time we bump into one another or see each other through the window, he blushes and runs the other way. It's starting to feel awkward.

I pulled into the spot and put the car in park. I check my pocketbook for my wallet, drop my keys in and grab my phone from the magnet on my dashboard as I get out and make my way through the parking lot and into the mall.

Shopping sucks! While still trying to keep my distance because of the whole covid thing, I maneuver my way through one store after another. I found an awesome shirt for Diesel and a sweater for Jacob. My dad is getting a new fishing pole and tackle box, and for my mom, I found this beautiful necklace from an antique stand. DJ, of course, has a ton of interactive learning toys.

Window shopping and maneuvering through the mall, I still need to find gifts for Dani and Nicki, and I'd like to get something special for Xander.

I walk up and down the aisles, glancing at lingerie outfits until I come across the cutest sexy Santa piece. I hold it up, trying to figure out how it would be worn. I throw it over my arm, along with a pair of jeans and a blouse, and I go in search of the changing room.

When I turn to get in line, I notice Xander up ahead and to the left. He holds up a couple of pairs of pants, and the woman points to the curtains on the right. When it's my turn, I realize he hasn't come out yet, so instead of going to the left where the women's changing rooms are, I beeline it to the left and slip between the curtain where Xander had entered.

"Hey, I'm..." he says, and I hush him by placing my hand over his mouth. His eyes go wide in surprise.

Fuck it!

I drop my hand down and lean forward. First, a small peck to show my intentions, then I lick his lip and push through. If I'm honest with myself, I've missed this, I've missed him. I step forward, causing his back to press against the wall. My hands come up to his cheeks, and I hold him.

I place my legs slightly apart, so his thigh rests against the seam of my pants. Our kiss becomes more heated when his arm reaches around. His hands rub me up and down my back. I bend my legs ever so slightly to rub back and forth on his leg. His hand comes down and grabs my ass, pulling me into him.

"Excuse me, excuse me?" The woman calls out, knocking on the side wall. I can't help but giggle as I pull back breathless.

I glance down at his crotch area, hard as hell. "I like these," I tell him and cup his hard-on through the pants. His head falls back, and he closes his eyes. I let go, turned, and stepped out from behind the curtain.

"Sorry," I tell the attendant, throw my pocketbook over my shoulder, and walk away with a big smile.

Damn, I still got it.

⁎ ⁎ ⁎

XANDER

Doesn't she understand? I'm going through hell, annoyed at all the little hints of her wanting to be with me over the years.

Yet here we are fighting. Why? Because I'm a virgin. I've built walls so I wouldn't get caught up with someone like her. But when we kiss, I step back and ask myself why?

I rub my face and place the slacks on the bench with the other things I plan to buy. I'm going home and taking a cold fucking shower. I'm done with shopping for today.

After another deep breath, I pull my phone out and send Kendra a message:

Me: *I can't do this as your teacher, mentor, or co-worker.*

She replies:

Kendra: *And what might THIS be?*

"I've been falling in love with her for years," I admit out loud to myself and realize I don't want to wait anymore. She is the one I want to lose my virginity to. The one I want to be with.

I begin to type my reply:

Me: *You win, Merry Christmas.*

She has been here patiently waiting all this time, giving me clues about how interested she is in me. This Christmas, I am going to get what I want, not like in the past. Always disappointed or alone. No, not this year. Things have changed. I have changed. For once in my life, I am going to go after what I want.

Who knew one kiss could change your whole outlook on things? On life?

Chapter Fourteen

Kendra

"LOOKS LIKE THE GANG'S all here," I say as I put the car in park. Xander and I climb out, and grab the bag from the back seat to meet him by the trunk to retrieve the gifts.

"I hope everyone likes what I got them," I say, tugging at one of the bags and grabbing another.

"I think you bought out the store," Xander says, laughing with his hands full of bags, as well.

We walk up the steps, and the door swings open, "Merry Christmas," my Mom says and waves us in. "Hi, Mom," we're greeted with the scent of the Prime Rib waffling through the air.

"Smells delicious, Mr. Johnson," Xander says in greeting with a kiss on her cheek.

"Thank you, thank you." She points toward the living room as we walk in and add the gifts under the tree.

Once everything is down, I turn and walk into the dining room, where the boys are.

"Ah, the man cave," I say, walking around the table and placing a kiss on my dad, Jacob, and Diesel's cheeks.

"You will find your man where there is food and drink." Dad laughs, holding up his bottle of Bud Light.

I stop, roll my eyes and watch while DJ pushes a toy car back and forth, making sounds.

"What's up, little man?" I kiss the top of his head. Xander shakes everyone's hand and pulls the chair at the end of the table to join them. I excuse myself to the kitchen to find my sisters.

During the holidays, we all usually help Mom in the kitchen. We all have our specialties. Mom makes the main course, Dani makes desserts, Nicki provides the holiday drinks, and I make the Antipasto salad and Mozzarella with tomato and basil platter.

"What are we drinking tonight?" I ask, bumping shoulders with Nicki. She raises her hands and shakes the aluminum container. "Candy Canes or Egg nog," She says, nodding toward the counter.

A plate with crushed candy canes sits beside the bottle of Strawberry vodka, creme de menthe, cranberry juice, and a tray of ice.

"Yummy!" Mom says, sipping and handing one over to me. "There is beer in the fridge for the men, as always."

I pull the fridge open and yell into the dining room, "Who needs a refill?" I grab three bottles and tuck one under my arm so I can grab my glass. Luckily, I made my salads before coming, so I had less work in the kitchen.

I place one beer in front of my dad, one in front of Diesel, and hand the last one to Xander as I sit on his lap.

Their conversation comes to a halt.

All eyes are questioning my actions.

"What? Geez, can't a girl have a little fun?" I sip my Candy Cane, then lick the rim as I lift myself from Xander's legs, laughing.

I sit next to him and giggle at how red his face is.

Seeing his reaction Diesel says, "Boy, you have no idea," and shakes his head.

Jacob chuckles, leaning back in his chair, agreeing uncomfortably.

"My girls are a handful," Dad says, unable to control his belly laughter.

"You have no idea," Xander mumbles, threading his fingers through his hair. I can't control myself and burst out laughing, spitting half my drink out in the process.

Everyone jumps with napkins, and we clean up the small mess, making room for the dinner to be brought in. I excuse myself and grab the salad and mozzarella platter from the fridge. Mom follows with the Prime Rib, Dani grabs the lasagna, and Nicki has the potatoes and vegetables.

We make small talk around the table while dad slices and serves.

"Looks wonderful, Mom," Dani says, lifting her fork, cutting a few pieces and placing them on DJ's plate. Nicki rounds the table, topping off everyone's drink, and then sits next to Diesel.

"I want to thank you all for having me," Xander nods toward my Mom and Dad.

"Well, Xander, you're part of the family. Where else would you be?" Mom winks, and I can think of a place I'd rather be.

In bed, with Xander between my legs. I reach down under the table and place my hand on his thigh. He glances slightly, trying not to be obvious, as I slide it closer to his cock.

Awkward? Not for me.

Chapter Fifteen

ONCE WE CLEAN UP THE table, we all move into the living room. Of course, we let DJ go first since it's almost his bedtime. He has the biggest smile as he unwraps his gifts, jumps up, gives a hug, and moves on to the next.

"You should have seen the mess he made this morning. We've been up since the ass crack of dawn," Dani says with a yawn. She gets up from the couch and cleans up all the wrapping paper.

DJ yells, "Thank you, everyone! Merry Christmas!" and climbs up on Jacob's lap, cuddling the stuffed dog with the long ears I gave him last year.

"DJ, who should go next," Mom asks since it's a tradition we started years ago, and it continues. One person opens at a time, so we can all appreciate the moment, and then they choose who opens next.

"You, Grandma!" he says, as he blows a kiss in her direction. She pretends to catch it and places it on her lips. I reached under the tree from the kitchen chair we brought in and dragged out all of Mom's presents.

Mom picks up and shakes each one by her ear and then opens it. When she gets to mine, I blush, feeling anxious. I hope she likes it. I found it at an antique shop. The owner said she has had the piece for many years but couldn't get rid of it because there are initials engraved on it.

It just so happens to be a D and J. I took it as a sign. This was meant for my mom.

D for David and J for Julie, my parents' names. The woman was thrilled and grateful for it to find a new home.

Once the box is open, she gasps, "Kendra, how did you…?"

Confused, I looked from her to the necklace and back again. What the fuck did I do?

"Mom?" I ask, getting up from my chair, walking around the couch, and putting my hand out. Taking the necklace, I place it around her neck. Once the clasp is locked in place, she lets her hair down and leans over to show my father.

"Kendra, I gave your mother a necklace just like this before we married." Mom walks to the mirror, "My god, it…it's exactly the same." She turns and hugs me with all her might.

"What happened to the necklace?" I wonder, is it possible this is her necklace?

"It was the winter before we got married. We were all up at TJ, the middle school. The one over on Fyke Lane." She reaches down and gets her drink.

After taking a sip, she continues, "Anyway, we were half crocked, and it was the middle of the night, and here we were sleigh riding on lunch trays and on garbage bags. When I got home and was getting ready for bed, I went to remove my necklace, but it was gone. I called your father frantically. We searched all my clothes and went back with flashlights to check the sleigh-riding hill. But we never found it."

My father reaches up and turns the necklace. "Pookie, it may have taken years, but we found it." His smile grows so big, "our initials are on the back."

Mom gasps takes my dad's cheeks in her hands, and kisses him.

I've never felt so proud of finally getting something right. Seeing the joy between them warms my heart.

We continued around the room until everyone was done. I got up to grab a garbage bag for all the wrapping paper, and Xander followed me into the kitchen.

"Um, I have another gift for you, but it's not here," he says as I turn and look over my shoulder.

"Oh?" I wonder what it could be. I bend down and reach for a bag, sticking my ass up and wiggling it.

He takes a step closer and places his hands on my hips. He whispers in my ear when I stand straight, "You have taken all my defenses away. You have ripped down all my walls. My gift to you is me. If you'll accept it."

With a spin on my heel, I wrap my arms around his neck, "Are you serious?" I ask and lick my upper lip. He nods.

"All of you?" I slide my right hand between us and cup his balls.

"Yes," he moans ever so lightly with his eyes closed.

"I have a gift at home for you, too." I explain, "Let's do what we have to do here and then see where the night takes us." I kiss him, step out of his arms and return to the living room to clean up.

Chapter Sixteen

XANDER

AFTER WE SAY GOODNIGHT, I hold Kendra's hand and descend the steps from her parents' house. She truly doesn't realize what an amazing woman she is. I can't keep my eyes off of her. My heart beats because of her.

All the years growing up feeling alone, it was worth it to bring me to her. The only decent foster family I had was my last. I was sixteen, and Margie took me under her wing. She spoke to me about all the trials and tribulations I've been through and will go through in the future.

Margie is the one who convinced me and explained how my virginity is sacred, how I should wait for the one woman I love and couldn't stand to live life without. That is Kendra for me.

I pull the car door open and close it behind her, then walk around the car and get in. We both buckle, and the engine turns over.

"Are you okay?" She asks, checking her rearview and side mirrors.

"Nervous," I admit, but with her, I can be honest. I am not ashamed.

We are quiet the rest of the way home. Once we park, I pull the handle and meet her in front of the car.

"Your house or mine?" she asks, smiling from ear to ear.

I'm going to do this, going to make love to her. I may not be any good, but she is the one. It took one kiss for me to fall in love with her, and I knew if she would be patient with me, we one day would be together, and now that day has come.

"Up to you," I tell her as we walk up the sidewalk.

"Okay, yours." She says, releasing my hand and turning toward her steps. Confused, I stop and ask, "Where are you going?" She giggles, "to get your gift, silly. I'll be over in ten minutes." She slides the key into the lock and disappears inside.

I dash up the walkway and step into my apartment. Once inside, I glance around to make sure the living room isn't a mess, and then I check the bedroom. The bed is made good.

I use the bathroom, check my armpits to make sure I don't smell, and then brush my teeth. My nerves are a mess, but I want her. No, I need her because I love her.

A knock comes from the door, and sweat forms on my forehead.

All or nothing, here we go.

Chapter Seventeen

I OPEN THE DOOR. KENDRA has one arm on the door frame and the other on her hip. She's my drug of choice, my kryptonite.

"What's with the raincoat?" I ask, glancing past her to see if it has started snowing or raining.

"It's your wrapping paper," she says with a giggle. In one step, she raises her hand using her pointer finger along my chin and guides my attention to her face as she steps past.

My cock is already growing. There's something different. Her shoes. She put heels on, black, tall, thin heels. I close the door behind us, and when she stops to look over her shoulder, I can't help myself.

I spin her into my arms, and our lips collide. When she gasps, I take full advantage and slide my tongue in. She tastes minty fresh. My hands come up to her cheeks, and I pull her closer, loving everything she does to me.

Kendra makes me feel alive, every nerve ending, every muscle, every inch of my body wanting hers. I'm so horny I'm about to come in my pants.

We take a few steps down the hall, and I turn into the bedroom.

She pulls back ever so slightly. "Xander, I've wanted this for so long."

I kiss her right cheek, then her left. "I have as well, but I had to be sure."

Her head tilts, "Sure of what?"

"Kendra, you are the only one I want to be with. Not just yesterday, or today, forever." I admit staring into her eyes.

"Xander, I don't know what to say." A tear falls from her eye, and I use my thumb to wipe it away.

"No one has ever cared enough about me to wait. You have. You are still here wanting me after six years." She swallows hard, "Xander, if you aren't ready, we can wait. I'd wait another sixty years if that's what it would take."

And with those words, I know all my life choices were the right ones. All because they brought me to her.

We kiss long and hard. I step forward, causing the back of her legs to bump into the mattress. Her body tenses as she glances up to make sure this is truly what I want. I answer by kissing the tip of her nose.

"You have to be patient with me," I say with my forehead leaning against hers. She tilts her head and places soft kisses along my jawline, moving down as she removes my shirt, letting it fall to the floor.

My body tenses when her fingers undo the button and zipper of my jeans. With featherlight kisses, she makes her way to my left nipple and then sucks hard. I let my head fall back. God she's killing me.

"Kendra, I need…" I suck in a deep breath when she pushes my pants down past my ass, and I'm exposed. Hard as fuck, bare and pulsing.

"Xander, I've wanted you for six years. I don't want to play these tit-for-tat games anymore. I want you." she says, as she kisses me with passion. I find the belt loop of the raincoat and untie it. Then reach up and began to slide it off her shoulders.

When it hits the ground, I take in the Christmas lingerie Santa baby-doll chemise she is wearing.

The see-through red, the sheer floral lace fabric is trimmed with white feathers around the halter neck, and it has black lace-up between her breasts. She steps to the side and turns slowly, her ass plump, and god, she is beautiful.

"What do you think?" she asks, stepping into me and wrapping her arms around my neck.

"I think it's going to be a very merry Christmas," I tell her and plant my lips on hers. Her leg comes up and wraps around my thigh, causing her to fall back, pulling me down onto the bed.

As we roll over, our bodies intertwine. I feel like I can't get close enough to her. She rolls me over so I am lying underneath her, and sits up. I can feel the heat coming from her crotch. My dick twitches when I reach out and pull the black satin, undoing the lace-up between her breasts.

Leaning up, I lick and kiss the now exposed skin. The sounds coming from her have me losing my mind, literally going haywire. Every nerve ending in my body is on fire. She slides the straps over her shoulders and lets the material fall. My breathing is erratic, waiting for the next move.

"You are going to have to take control now," I whisper my confession. Her head tilts, "I got you, Xander, and I will never let you go."

"One kiss is all it took. I didn't need one hour or one night to understand how I felt. It took one kiss, and I was yours." She says, kissing her way up my torso.

"I told you once before I would give you all of me, so here I am," I tell her and lean down with a kiss.

"I love you, Kendra. I want this." I told her again. She becomes more passionate than before. A hunger, a need, has us both moaning. With every touch, I feel myself growing thicker and harder.

I lie back and let her settle her entrance above me. The heat coming from her has me ready.

"Are you sure?" she asks, lowering herself slowly. I nod, close my eyes and let her take me.

Holy. Fuck.

She moves up and down my shaft her hands on my chest for support. Slow then fast, fuck this is insane. She moans, "Xander, you feel so good."

Mother of God. Fireworks. She is so warm, wet, and tight. It's so much better than my hand.

I'm blind. I swear I'm blind!

She moves up and down again, and I explode, "Keni!" I screamed because I had no time for anything else. She pumps a few more times and lowers herself to the side.

I place my forearm over my eyes. Embarrassed, I had came so quickly, but oh my god, that was the most intense feeling I have ever had.

Her head on my shoulder whispers, "Merry Christmas!"

I turn and look at her dead in the face, "You are mine."

Giggling, she leans over my shoulder, "Possessive, I like it," and kisses my cheek as she wraps her arm over my stomach, and I take a few deep breaths.

***

KENDRA

It may have been quick, but god, I needed that. I kiss his cheek one last time before resting my head on his shoulder to fall asleep.

He has given me the most wonderful gift. He gave me him.

I'm so glad I stuck it out and waited for him. He is everything I've ever wanted. Our personalities blend well together, and we love the same things. We couldn't get along better if we tried. Don't get me wrong, we have disagreements, but once he realizes I'm right, all is good.

If I think about it, we have dated for the last couple of years. I glance up and admire his face. He had fallen asleep.

"I love you, Xander. Merry Christmas." I gently press my lips against his jawbone and rest my head on his shoulder. His arm pulls me in a little closer, I feel a kiss on the top of my head, and he says, "I love you more."

Chapter Seventeen

FEATHER-LIKE KISSES along my side have me squirming awake. I glance down, covering my mouth to hide my morning breath.

"Well, good morning," I let my fingers ruffle his hair.

Before taking my nipple in his mouth, he looks up and says, "Morning."

My head falls back, and I let out a soft moan. Now, this is how a woman should be woken up every day. God Damn.

He kisses over my stomach and down until he spreads my legs further apart. After he nestles in between my thighs, he blows and licks, causing my insides to ignite. His tongue moves up and down, spreading me wider. When he coats the nub, I spring up, "I need you."

He chuckles, crawling up my body for a kiss. I wrap my leg around his naked thigh and tighten the muscle to help guide him in. He doesn't hesitate and thrusts deep.

"Fuck, I don't know why I waited so long to feel so good," he admits, pulling out and sliding in again and again. Getting a little harder and faster. This is better than last night. Not that I was disappointed, but it was rather quick for his first time.

"I can do this all day with you." He thrust forward, and his forearm muscles tightened, holding him above me. His hips were circling, "I think I've created a monster," I say between breaths, "You feel amazing."

I rake my nails down his back, and he cries out. I let out a moan and throw my arm up over my head, opening my mouth in a silent scream as he pumps in and out, and I meet him with every thrust.

My climax builds, and I know I have to let go, "Xander, I'm coming!" I pull him into me and ride out my orgasm. Feeling his seed fill me, fuck, we haven't used protection.

Screw it. I don't care. I've waited six years for this man to be inside me. If I were to get pregnant, I'd deal with it.

He passionately kisses me before pulling out and falling to the side.

"Kendra, only you could make me feel so alive and dead at the same time. I'm exhausted." He pulls the sheet over and fixes his pillow. We cuddle for a little while. Then I get up to make us something to eat and drink while he rests.

Coffee, I definitely need coffee.

While the coffee pot brews, I take my phone from the table. I've missed three calls from Nicki and two from Dani. What the hell?

I call Nicki. It rings two times before she picks it up.

"Where the fuck have you been?" She yells into the phone.

"I'm at Xander's. What's the problem?" I snap back at her.

"It's Dad. I'm sorry to be the one to have to tell you, but he's in the hospital."

"What? What happened?" I can feel all the blood drain from my face, and I get light-headed, so I take a seat on the kitchen chair as Xander walks in.

His smile turns to fear the minute he sees my face. He rushes over and falls to his knees in front of me. "What's wrong?"

"Nicki, what happened? Where is he?" I ask, needing to know so I can get dressed and be by his side. My father is our rock. He holds this family together through thick and thin. We can't lose him.

"He had a heart attack this morning. He's in Hackensack. I'll see you soon." She hangs up before I can say another word. Xander takes the phone from me, and the tears begin to fall.

"Keni Honey, what's wrong?" he asks, taking my hands in his.

"We have to get to Hackensack. It's my dad." I throw my arms around his neck and squeeze. He holds me to him for a moment then gets up and runs into the bedroom. He brings me a pair of sweatpants and a t-shirt, then returns to dress himself.

"I'll drive," he takes my hand and leads us out the door to my car.

I'm numb. This can't be happening.

Daddy.

Chapter Eighteen

WE ARRIVE AT THE HOSPITAL and enter the main doors. When it is our turn at the desk, we are greeted by a young man, "Can I help you?"

I look around, lost. Xander steps in, "David Johnson was brought in this morning. We are family." The gentleman clicks on the computer and then makes a phone call.

"You can take the elevators up to the fourth floor. Someone will be waiting to assist you there." He hands Xander two visitor passes, and we go.

When the elevator doors open, Dani, Jacob, DJ, Nicki, and Diesel are all sitting in a waiting room. My sisters leap from the chairs, and we all hug. They pull me to the side and explain. Dad had a minor heart attack. They performed emergency surgery, everything went fine, and Mom is with him now.

"I'm so sorry. I left my phone in the kitchen. I'm so sorry," I repeat over and over again as the tears fall. Xander comes and wraps me in his arms, "this is not your fault. You did nothing wrong. You are here now, and that is what matters." I nod, understanding, but it doesn't prevent the guilt from settling in my stomach.

About a half hour later, Mom comes down the hall. I spring from the chair and run toward her with open arms. "I'm so sorry, Mommy."

She squeezes me tight, "Keni, everything is fine. He had the surgery and will be in and out of it for a few hours."

We walk toward my family, and Mom updates everyone. Xander comes and stands next to me, taking my hand in his. He is being amazing, and his words and support are holding me together.

"Let's go get some food from the café. I can use a coffee." Nicki says, grabbing her and Dani's pocketbooks from the chairs.

None of us really eat. We sit around a table and pass glances back and forth.

"Mom, how did this happen?" I bravely ask, knowing my father can never sit still. He is up and doing something if he isn't telling a story.

"Well, umm..." She glances from one face to another and stops at me since I asked the question.

"We were in bed, and well..." My eyes pop open. Holy fuck.

"Okay, Okay. I get it." I hold my hand up, stopping her from saying any more.

Diesel starts to chuckle, and it starts the whole table laughing.

Then he says, "Fucking Johnson's," which causes us to laugh even more.

Mom and Dad going at it hot and heavy was not an image I needed to have in my head.

About an hour later, we all returned to the floor and were allowed to go into Dad's room.

When Mom stepped through the door, he reached his arm out for her to take his hand.

"Julie, you rocked my world." He mumbles with a smile. She swats at him and says, "I tried to kill you," they both laugh. It's at that moment I am reminded of how grateful I am to have the family I have. We may joke and play, but we will always have each other's backs.

Chapter Nineteen

BETWEEN SPENDING EVERY available minute in Xander's arms, I've been cleaning, cooking, and helping Mom set the house up for Dad. Not that there is much to do, but we did move the Christmas tree and make more room in the living room, where he will rest in his recliner until it's time for him to go to bed. You'd never know Christmas was just three days ago.

"Any plans for the new year?" Mom asks, rinsing the last dish in the sink.

"To be honest, I haven't even thought about it," I say, with a shrug of my shoulders, placing another tin of food in the fridge. The doctors say Dad will have his discharge papers in the morning; other than following up and taking his medications, he should be fine.

"Nicki mentioned the Wig Wam. Maybe we can all go and spend it together?" She puts the dish in the dish drain and grabs a paper towel to dry her hands.

"I'm up for it. You think Dad will be?" I wonder about taking a seat at the kitchen table.

"It was his idea," she says.

"Then it's settled, New Year's Eve at the bar with the family." I hold up my cup of coffee. She clicks hers against it and takes the seat across from me.

"So, how are things?" She fiddles with the napkin resting on the table in front of her.

"Things?" I place my cup down and sit back in the chair.

"You and Xander have been inseparable. Surprised he isn't here now," she giggles.

"Things are good, kind of what I've always wanted and have been waiting for." I smile, thinking of how long it took us to get here.

"You look happy, and that is all we ever wanted for our girls."

I get up from my chair, walk around the table and hug her. "With Dad on the mend, I couldn't be happier." Then I turn and lift the faucet to wash my mug in the sink.

"I'm going to head home. Dani is going with you to get Dad in the morning, right?" I confirm, and she nods.

"Okay, call me if you need anything. Make sure to hog the bed tonight because he'll be back tomorrow." I joke, blow her a kiss, walk through the hall past the stairs and out the front door.

When I pull up to our apartments, I notice Xander's light on in the living room. I pull my phone from my pocket and shoot him a text, letting him know I am home.

The three dots appear, and then they are gone. No reply.

I slide my key in the lock and enter, throwing my jacket on the hook and placing my keys on the small table before heading into the living room. I plop down on the couch, rest my head, and close my eyes.

It's been a hell of a few days. I'm running on empty.

Chapter Twenty

I'M WOKEN UP BY THE sound of pots and pans clanging together. I sit up from the couch I must have passed out on and look over my shoulder.

"Morning, I didn't mean to wake you," Xander says, sliding pancakes on a plate. Everything smells delicious. The coffee is brewed, and some bacon is sizzling in the pan.

"Good morning. What time did you get here?" I ask, yawning and stretching my arms above my head.

"About a half hour after you got home, I couldn't bear to wake you. You haven't slept in days." He forks the bacon from the frying pan and puts it on the plate holding the eggs and pancakes.

I step up behind him and wrap my arms across his stomach, "You better be careful. A girl can get used to this." I joke and kiss the bare skin of his shoulder.

"Dani called. They are on the way to get your Dad. She said Mom doesn't want any company today. Let's let them settle, and they will see us tomorrow." I take the plate he holds out and retreats to the table with it.

He brings the pot of coffee and fills our cups.

"Mom was talking yesterday about New Year's Eve. Do you have any plans?" I lift the fork to my mouth and glance up. His face blushes. What the fuck is that about?

"Whatever you want to do is fine, but I'm the only one you are kissing at midnight," he says, shoving a big piece of pancake into his mouth. I can't help laughing.

"You're the only one I want to kiss, so there!" I pull the fork back and fling some scrambled eggs in his direction. The commotion erupts, and the laughter fills the apartment as he gets up and chases me around the sofa and into the bedroom.

We fall onto the bed, kissing when the alarm on his phone goes off.

"Shit, I forgot about the teacher's seminar." Leaning up so he could run his fingers through his hair.

"You go to work, and I promise, we will bring in the New Year with a bang." He smirks, kisses me quickly, and then jumps from the bed and leaves the room.

I can't believe tonight is New Year's Eve and tomorrow is New Year's Day already.

*** * ***

XANDER

I have everything set. We will all be at the Wig Wam for food and drinks and maybe a little dancing. I grab the keys to Kendra's car and beeline to the parking lot. The store is only open for another twenty minutes, and it takes me fifteen to get there.

I turned on Palisades Avenue and left onto Cedar Lane, glancing at the clock and the rearview mirrors. I step on the gas.

When I pull into the Bergen Town Center, I leap from the car and dash across the parking lot.

Yanking on the glass doors, I enter and am greeted by the sales associate.

"Is it ready?" I huff out, feeling the excitement build.

She nods and brings me to the counter to reveal Kendra's gift. I hope she loves it as much as I love her.

Chapter Twenty One

THE WIG WAM IS CROWDED, but luckily Nicki reserved the back table and booth for us. When we walk through, we are greeted by all the regulars. As we reach the end of the bar, Nicki comes around and wraps her arms around me.

"Happy New Year, kiddo. It's going to be a great year," she says. I'm a little confused as to why she thinks it will be great, but okay. Let's drink!

We each get a drink, I kiss Diesel on the cheek, and Xander shakes his hand with a nod. I turn to go to the table where Dani and Jacob are sitting with my mother and father.

"This is just another reason why I love you," Xander says, taking my free hand in his.

"Why is that?" I ask, placing my drink on the table and letting him help remove my jacket.

"Family, you all are an inspiration for me. It's what I want someday," he says, reaching out to shake my father's hand and kiss mom on the cheek. He then turns and does the same with Jacob and Dani.

"Family is what life is all about," my father says, holding a pint glass.

"I'll drink to that," we all say and laugh at how in sync we are.

"Dad, should you be drinking?" I ask, wiping my lip and raising my eyebrow at the stubborn man.

"One or two won't hurt me. It's your mother I have to worry about." Mom lightly smacks his arm and then kisses him on his cheek.

"We are not having that conversation again, please. I had nightmares, for crying out loud." Dani says, covering her eyes, embarrassed that my parents still get hot and heavy between the sheets and caused my father's heart attack.

I can't help but laugh. The conversation goes around the table for a while until they announce ten minutes to midnight. Most of the patrons get refills while the rest of us get up from our seats and crowd around the dance floor where the big screen television shows the ball that drops in New York City.

To think I've lived here my whole life and have never gone to watch the ball drop. I mean, it's a twenty-minute drive from Teaneck, maybe next year.

"It's finally time!" Nicki yells, pushing her and Diesel through the small crowd to join the family.

10...

9...

8...

Xander steps in front of me and goes down on one knee. My eyes pop wide open. What the fuck is he doing?

7...

"One Kiss and I fell in love with you," he pulls a velvet box from his side and holds it up.

6...

"Kendra Johnson, I watched you grow up before my eyes…"

5…

"from being a student to becoming a co-worker and, more importantly, my best friend."

4….

"Will you grow old with me?"

3…

"Will you take this ring?"

2…

"and marry me?"

Tears overflow, the man I've loved forever wants to spend forever with me.

1 !!!!

"YES!!" I grab his cheeks, pulling him up for a kiss.

This is not just any ordinary kiss. This is One Kiss I know we will both remember for the rest of our lives.

After all the congratulations and Happy New Year's settle down, we return to the table. Xander removes the ring from the box, and I hold out my left hand.

He slowly slides it onto my ring finger as I admire the design.

Three sparkling diamonds meet in the center of a white and rose gold infinity symbol. The smile spreading across my face is unstoppable.

"It's beautiful," I reach out to show my family, and they all compliment how beautiful it is.

"And just so you know, I asked your parents' permission three weeks ago. We have their blessings," he whispers in my ear.

He went old school and asked for my hand. How precious is that?

The End

Epilogue

DANIELLE AND JACOB continue to live across the street from The Johnson Sisters' childhood home. They are expecting their second child. DJ (David Jacob) is excited to meet his little brother in the fall, and is thrilled to be starting school. No, he won't be going away to school like Jacob had to. Instead, both Dani and Jacob will walk DJ every morning down the street to the corner and wave goodbye, then meet him there in the afternoon when school is over.

Nicollette and Diesel have completed the renovations on his grandmother's house and have started decorating the nursery. That's right, Nicki is knocked up. We all knew it was bound to happen sooner rather than later with the amount of sex those two have. They are nervous yet anxious to meet the little bug, especially since she is three days past her due date. Nicki claims if he/she doesn't come soon, she is going to beat the daylights out of Diesel for doing this to her. I'd look out, Diesel! Pregnant or not, a Johnson is true to their word.

Kendra and Xander are enjoying married life. They had a small elegant wedding with just the family. Then they took off on a three-week cruise. Since they've been back, Keni was awarded the job of her dreams. She is now teaching first and second graders while Xander returns to Fairleigh Dickinson University.

They applied to adopt a child and were approved shortly after purchasing a house over in Bergenfield. The official adoption paperwork and records will be signed at the end of the month. Margaret (Margie, we call her in honor of Xander's foster mother) will officially be theirs, and in just a few short months, another baby will be born.

That's right, ladies and gentlemen, three Johnson sisters, are all having babies at the same time. Oh Boy!

Through thick and thin, live, love, and laugh because family always comes first.

About Elaine Marie

I'M A TRUE JERSEY GIRL at heart. I currently reside in the northern part of the beautiful Garden State—New Jersey—with my hubby, three amazing children, and our dogs and cats.

In my spare time, I can be found rooting for my favorite football and hockey teams. Other than my family, my passion is reading and creating amazing stories that captivate the heart.

Contact Elaine Marie

Facebook:

https://m.facebook.com/EMarieBooks/

Twitter:

@EMarieBooks

Instagram:

@ElaineMarieAuthor

TikTok:

@EMarieBooks

Email:

ElaineMarieAuthor@gmail.com

Books By Elaine Marie

Déjà vu[1]
Snow Kisses[2]
Sunshine Kisses[3]
Falling for the Dare The Falling Series Book 1[4]
Falling for the Past The Falling Series Book 2[5]
Living[6]
Because I Can The Because Trilogy Book 1[7]
Because I Won't The Because Trilogy Book 2[8]
TTYL ParisThe FYI < 3 Series Book 1[9]
L8R London The FYI < 3 Series Book 2[10]
WTF Venice The FYI < 3 Series Book 3[11]

---

1. http://amzn.com/B07GDVY91W

2. http://amzn.com/B01N1RZH2I

3. https://www.amazon.com/dp/B0875M4VZP

4. http://Amzn.com/B07RB2G6S9

5. http://Amzn.com/B07RB2G6S9

6. http://amzn.com/B06XK4BWYH

7. http://amzn.com/B01LYI56O2

8. http://amzn.com/B07GC634S6

9. http://amzn.com/B07D7GFH1J

10. http://amzn.com/B07D857Y2M

<u>OMG Cabo The FYI < 3 Series Book 4</u>[12]

11. http://amzn.com/B07GGBFGWB

12. http://amzn.com/B07HGJP83J